Willie and Uncle Bill

AMY SCHWARTZ

Holiday House / New York

For Jacob and Aunt Debbie,
the real Willie and Uncle Bill

Copyright © 2012 by Amy Schwartz
All Rights Reserved
HOLIDAY HOUSE is registered in the U.S. Patent and Trademark Office.
Printed and Bound in April 2013 at Kwong Fat Offset Printing Co., Ltd.,
Dongguan City, China.
The text typeface is Hank.
The artwork was created with gouache and pen and ink on Rives BFK.
www.holidayhouse.com
3 5 7 9 10 8 6 4 2

Library of Congress Cataloging-in-Publication Data
Schwartz, Amy.
Willie and Uncle Bill / Amy Schwartz. — 1st ed.
p. cm.
Summary: When Willie's Uncle Bill comes to babysit,
they have excellent adventures making icky stew,
getting a haircut at Hair by Pierre, and jamming
with a band.
ISBN 978-0-8234-2203-6 (hardcover)
[1. Uncles—Fiction. 2. Babysitters—Fiction.] I. Title.
PZ7.S406Wil 2012
[E]—dc22
2011007274

ISBN 978-0-8234-2907-3 (paperback)

The Haircut

The doorbell rang three times.

Uncle Bill had come to watch Willie.

Willie answered the door. He was wearing checked pants and a big striped shirt.

"Wow," Uncle Bill said.

"Bill," Willie's mother said. "Make sure you keep a good eye on Willie today."

Willie's mother kissed Willie good-bye.

"Willie," Uncle Bill said.
"Please play quietly
while I make lunch."
Willie played quietly.

Then he went into
the bathroom and
locked the door.

Uncle Bill decided to make tacos.
First he put the meat on the stove.

Then he turned on the radio.   He danced a little dance.

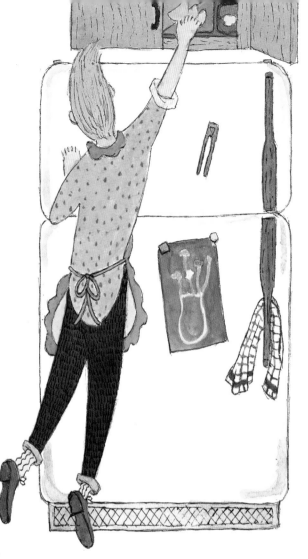

He found the taco shells
and the taco sauce.
Uncle Bill chopped
up the lettuce,
the tomatoes,
and the onions.
He grated the cheese.

Then he made chocolate
pudding for dessert.

"Willie!" Uncle Bill called. "Lunch!"

"Willie!"
Uncle Bill jiggled the doorknob to the bathroom.
"Willie! Open the door!"

Willie opened the door. He was wearing the same checked pants.
He was wearing the same striped shirt.
But something was very different.
Willie's hair was different. "I cut it myself," Willie said.

"Well," Uncle Bill said.
Uncle Bill picked up the scissors.
He snipped here, and he snipped there.

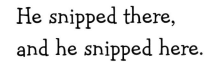

He snipped there,
and he snipped here.

Uncle Bill stood back.
"I think we need help," he said.
Uncle Bill helped Willie on with his red sweatshirt.

They walked a block and a half.
Then they entered Hair—by Pierre.
"Oh, la la!" Pierre said.
He pointed to a big chair.
Willie climbed in.

Pierre put a dark green apron on Willie.
Then he snipped here, and he snipped there.
He snipped there, and he snipped here.

"Voilà," Pierre said. Willie looked in the mirror.
His hair was short. It was very, very short.
"It's very... Now," Uncle Bill said.

Willie and Uncle Bill walked the block and a half home.
Uncle Bill helped Willie off with his sweatshirt.

They had tacos for lunch.

Willie's mother came home before dark.

"Hello, Bill," she said. "Where's Willie?"

"Before you say hello to Willie," Uncle Bill said,

"there's just one short . . .

. . . one very, very short . . .

. . . thing you should know."

Icky Stew

The doorbell rang three times.
Uncle Bill had come to watch Willie.
"Bill," Willie's mother said,
"*please*, just don't do anything I wouldn't do."
She kissed Willie good-bye.

"Willie," Uncle Bill said,
"let's make Icky Stew."
He took a shiny copper pan down
off the wall and put it on the stove.

"What's our first ingredient?"
Uncle Bill said.
"Chocolate!" Willie said.
"Brilliant!"
Uncle Bill unwrapped
a chocolate bar with almonds
and put it in the pan.
He turned up the heat.

Then Uncle Bill opened the refrigerator.

"Willie, what next?"

"Tuna salad!" Willie said.

"Awesome."

"And Worcestershire sauce!" Willie said.

"And mustard!

And liverwurst!"

Willie and Uncle Bill stirred
the tuna salad,
Worcestershire sauce,

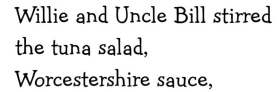

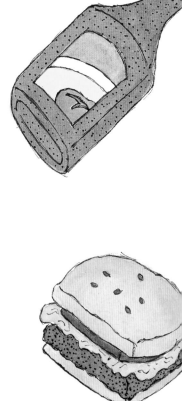

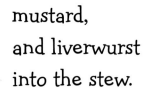

mustard,
and liverwurst
into the stew.

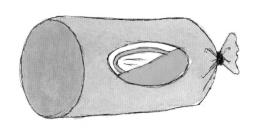

"Is it Icky Stew yet?" Willie asked.

"No," Uncle Bill said.

Willie and Uncle Bill stirred in: a tablespoon of pepper, some ketchup, half of a leftover hamburger, and a scoop of ice cream—pistachio.

"Now," Uncle Bill said. "It's Icky Stew."

Uncle Bill took a tiny, tiny taste. He held out the spoon to Willie.

"No thank you," Willie said.

Uncle Bill poured the Icky Stew
into a bowl with a cover.
"What should we do with the leftovers?"
Uncle Bill said.
"Let's go for a walk.
Maybe we'll find some customers."

Uncle Bill helped Willie into his red sweatshirt.

Willie, Uncle Bill, and the Icky Stew headed down the block.
The dog walker said hello.
"Would your pups like some Icky Stew?" Willie asked.
"Not today," the dog walker said.

The garbageman waved to Willie.
"Can we offer you a snack?"
Uncle Bill said.
"No thanks," the garbageman said.

Willie and Uncle Bill turned onto the boardwalk.
Seagulls with big orange beaks were flying everywhere.

Willie and Uncle Bill sat on a bench.
Uncle Bill put the Icky Stew down beside him. He took off the cover.
A seagull landed on the plastic container. He took a taste.

Then another seagull landed,
and then another, and then another.
"I think we've found our customers,"
Uncle Bill said.
Soon the Icky Stew was all gone.
Uncle Bill looked at the sun.
"Yipes!" he said. "Time to get home."

He helped Willie out of his sweatshirt.

Five minutes later, Willie's mother came home. She put down her bags.

"What have you two been up to?" she asked. "Anything exciting?"

"Oh, we didn't do much," Uncle Bill said.

"In fact, you could say . . ." Uncle Bill crossed his arms.

"We just spent the afternoon . . .

. . . stewing around!"

The Outing

The doorbell rang three times.

Uncle Bill had come to watch Willie.

"Willie's all ready in his pj's," Willie's mother said.

"It would be good, Bill, if you two had a peaceful evening."

She kissed Willie good-bye.

Willie and Uncle Bill played with Willie's trains.

They read a few books.

They launched a few rocket ships.
Then they ran out of toys.

Uncle Bill opened the window.
"It's a beautiful evening," he said.
"Too beautiful to stay inside."
Uncle Bill helped Willie
into his red sweatshirt.

Willie and Uncle Bill walked two blocks to the subway.
They climbed down the stairs.
"Where are we going?" Willie asked.
"You'll see," Uncle Bill said.

The subway went into a tunnel.
It went over a bridge.
"This is our stop," Uncle Bill said.

Willie and Uncle Bill started walking.

Willie could hear rock-and-roll music.

The longer they walked, the louder it got.

They stopped in front of a yellow brick garage.

The music was very loud.

"Here we are," Uncle Bill shouted.

Uncle Bill pounded on the door three times.

"Willie," Uncle Bill yelled to Willie. "It's *The Purple Tomatoes*."

A *Purple Tomato* opened the garage door.
He had red hair and an electric guitar.
"Welcome!" he shouted.

Willie and Uncle Bill sat down on a patched sofa.
Three men and a woman wearing crazy pants
were playing electric guitars and drums.
They were singing very loudly.

Willie and Uncle Bill
tapped their feet
and nodded their heads.
They ate tortilla chips
and guacamole.

The man with the red hair took off his guitar.
He handed it to Uncle Bill.
"Should I?" Uncle Bill asked Willie.
"Yes!" Willie said.

Uncle Bill played a song with *The Purple Tomatoes*.
He sang and he screamed.
He held the guitar up over his head,
and he slid on his knees across the floor.

"Your turn," Uncle Bill said. He gave Willie the guitar.
Willie joined *The Purple Tomatoes*. He strummed the guitar.
It let out a mighty squeal. *So did Willie.*
"Excellent!" Uncle Bill shouted.
"Quite!" yelled the man with red hair.

The *Purple Tomatoes* sang and shouted and yelled and stomped.
So did Willie.
The woman with the crazy pants did a split. So did Willie.

Uncle Bill looked at his watch.

"Jeepers!" he shouted. "It's late!"

Willie and Uncle Bill jogged the four blocks back to the subway.

They rode the subway over the bridge

and through the tunnel.

They sprinted the two blocks home.
Uncle Bill helped Willie off with his sweatshirt.

Willie's mother came home. She took off her shoes.
"Well, I hope you two had a nice, quiet evening," she said.
"How did you entertain yourselves?"
"Well, we did have a nice evening," Uncle Bill said.
He winked at Willie.
"And Willie was *quite* entertaining."